NEJMA

BY NAYYIRAH WAHEED

ISBN-10: 14944993322
ISBN-13: 978-1494493325

to you.
my people. of color.

you are an altar of stars.
remember this.
always.
do not ever forget this.

NEJMA
BY NAYYIRAH WAHEED

i am writing this book.
ii am writing a daughter.

— nejma (nejii)

i sang a god alive for you.

give me a moment…
i am adjusting the roses in my tongue.

— the rose farm

the night west of the ocean.
i fell asleep
between
your body and your soft unbody.

— zejune

the sun cleanses itself.
i cleanse myself.
for both of us.
it is morning.

— wuḍū

some words. the way they look at you…

you are a private gold.

— gold

you are a flood in my hands.

i want
work that is a relentless
oasis.

i was every light for you.

can you feel my prayers.
there and.
there and.
there.

— pilgrimage

you smell like love.

and
all this
red sand.
black air.
and
loose life. falling into
my skin.

— snow island

you and the poems have a lot to talk about.

put some honey and sea water by your bed.
acknowledge. that your being needs sweetness and cleansing.
that it is sore.
that you are. soft.

— orishas

there was an evening in what you said.

i wanted the wanting.

there are poems. before the poem.

you were three years of water.

something.
is migrating up my neck.

here.

among the red pepper blood trees.
i feel
my life
in
my
mouth.

the fire.
that's not where i burn from.

weep the light.

grieve. so that you can be free to feel something else.

let the poems have you.

NEJMA

BY NAYYIRAH WAHEED

early.
while the sun is still white.
i pick the pink leaves.
i heat the water until it becomes milk.
i search for the cinnamon juice i made yesterday.
and i find it.
next to the lemons soaking in rose molasses.

when words take off their clothes. for me.
so i can write. them
exactly. as they are.

— skin

yes. yes i do. have the right to be this lush and neverending.

the swarm of this bright. fat. oil.
rinsing my back.
turning my thighs into sleep.

— the red oil

and i heard her say, ‘you are afraid of love. but love is not afraid of you.’

drop a name in the water.
drop a name in the water.
and a name in the water.
drop another name in the water.
and another.
and another.
and another.
and another.
and another.
and another.
and another.
and another.
and another.
and another.
until
there are no more bodies in your body.

— the rivering

(all i can do is rest.)
my body is in the middle of a poem.

there is prayer in poem.

when i am writing
i am praying.

all the prayers that are too soft.
too young.
too old.
to say.

with grace.
with grace.
with grace.

you
will bare
and
you will sieve.

with grace.

— husk

sometimes
i smell my parents
on my words.
and i weep.

we need to share our wars.

NEJMA

BY NAYYIRAH WAHEED

our tragedy begins humid.
in a humid classroom.
with a humid text book. breaking into us.
stealing us from ourselves.
one poem. at a time.

it begins with shakespeare.

the hot wash.
the cool acid. of
dead white men and women. people.

each one a storm.

crashing. into our young houses.
making us islands. easy isolations.
until we are so beleaguered and
swollen
with a definition of poetry that is white skin and
not us.
that we tuck our scalding. our soreness.
behind ourselves and
learn
poetry.
as trauma. as violence. as erasure.
another place we do not exist.
another form of exile
where we should praise. honor. our own starvation.

NEJMA

BY NAYYIRAH WAHEED

the little bits of langston. phyllis wheatley.
and
angelou during black history month. are the crumbs. are the minor boats.
that give us slight rest.

to be waterdrugged into rejecting the nuances of
my own bursting
extraordinary
self.
and to have
this
be
called
education.

to take my name out of my name.
out of where my native poetry lives. in me.
and
replace it with keats. browning. dickson. wolf. joyce. wilde. wolfe. plath. bronte. hemingway. hughes. byron. frost. cummings. kipling. poe. austen. whitman. blake. longfellow. wordsworth. duffy. twain. emerson. yeats. tennyson. auden. thoreau. chaucer. thomas. raliegh. marlowe. burns. shelley. carroll. elliot…

(what is the necessity of a black child being this high off of whiteness.)

and so. we are here. brown babies. worshipping. feeding. the glutton that is white literature. even after it dies.

— the hot wash

(years later. the conclusion:

shakespeare is relative.

white literature is relative.

that we are force fed the meat of
an animal
that our bodies will not recognize. as inherent nutrition.
is not relative.
is inert.)

your novels.
the classic novels of a minutia. i have no interest in.
pale. in comparison to the novels of my world.
the novel of my mother.
the novels of my grandparents.
the articulate novels of how my people walk down a street.
the novels i have been reading my whole life.

— classic

the eye room.
the arm room.
the small room in the feet.
the lung room.
the teeth room.
the tight room of the hair.
these are. our. rooms.
this is where. we. become the soft sharks of our literature.

— the writing rooms (black libraries)

there is a small bee in my writing.
it is a small gift. from the ancestors.
to keep my work pure.

— bee

to be black.
and
a moon.

— light

(up late.)
making a flower stew. (otherwise known as a poem.)

there is no healthier drug than creativity.

(all the places
the darkest light
lives in you.)

— bioluminescence (the biology of light)

poetry.
is an infusion
of
scale
and feather.
bruise
and mist.

you are the thing.
that comes from your
soul.

the poem.
the one. that is running through your life.
pay attention.
to that poem.

'as you are.' says the universe.
'after...' you answer.
'as you are.' says the universe.
'before...' you answer.
'as you are.' says the universe.
'when...' you answer.
'as you are.' says the universe.
'how...' you answer.
'as you are.' says the universe.
'why...' you answer.
'because
you are happening now.
right now.
right at this moment
and
your happening
is beautiful.
the thing that both keeps me alive
and
brings me to my knees.
you don't even know how breathtaking you
are.
as you are.' says the universe through tears.

— as you are | you are the prayer

you.
everything about you. comes so naturally to me.

(may i tell you something.)
the words.
they are in love with you.

flowerworks.

how does the sea remember me. every time.

this prayer.
this prayer.
this prayer.
'elder mandela.
here is my heart to place under yours.
as
right now
you are slow breaths
and
low eye.
all that strength you made from horror.
from
a jail cell. made of your mother's island.
i return some to you.
here.
are my legs.
my arms.
my voice.

madiba.
ninety four years
is
many lives.
is many bones to go through.
many walks through the sun.
many hearts to shed.
many stars of joy to comb through your hair.
a lot of time
to drink.
let us hold you now.
let us warm the water for your skin.
let our youth be your comfort.
we have seen how your feet danced.
know.
that we have committed
your rhythm.
your song.
you. to memory.
our weeping
is
all hope and fresh mourning.

we know what the ancestors sound like
when they come.
when
they are ready for you.
madiba.
if you have done
what
you came to do.
if
you are finished transcribing your soul into humanity.
we will
have our cloth ready.
our flowers ready.
our songs in our mouths ready.
our feet and all the drums ready.
our fresh water.
our spirits.
ready.
to
walk
you
home.
ashé.'

— watching over madiba (june. 23, 2013. 6:07 p.m. est, usa)

NEJMA

BY NAYYIRAH WAHEED

and what happened
when you left
madiba.
all the water started to weep.
and
the lands ate our feet.
and
africa had to keep
the
sky from jumping into her lap from
grief.

what happened
madiba
when you left.
we got out the pots.
and put our laughter into our teeth.
and
prepared meals. so we could release you.
let you go.
as
we ground the seed.
blew the spice.
stirred
you into being gone. we ate raw petal. sniffed cinnamon sticks to perfume your leaving
our bodies.

what happened
when
you left
madiba.
they
came to
dissect your body.
wanting us
to
smile and nod while they plucked your eyes into
their pockets for later.
for
the time when they will make your name. a science. a war. against us.
(madiba. you are a different grief.
for us.)
what happened when you
left
madiba.
your people.
we

softened. and broke. and kneeled over in pain. and sang. and threw ourselves against the walls. against each other. and hid. and caved. and opened. and tossed ourselves into work. and danced. and shrank. and closed. and ate. and bled. and held on. and ignored. and accepted. and lied. and laughed. and created. and undid. and drank. and drugged. and loved something. someone. somewhere. ourselves. fiercer. and hated. something. someone. somewhere. ourselves. fiercer. and swam. and rejected. and yearned. and distanced. and clawed. and touched. and some of us will disown you. because you hurt too much. some of us will have to say your name for a year. before we are able to sleep.

— what is left (the day after you have gone)

i have been eating flowers.
drinking honey. every day. for every meal.
all this sweetness
eases my blood from missing you, madiba.

— coping (grief poems)

sometimes i want to say it.
and there is nothing in english. that will say it.

there is oil in the water.

i am drunk from all the honey.
i have been drinking. for days straight.
every night i eat water
until i fall asleep.
i am trying to remember you, madiba.
and
let you go
at
the same time.
i am throwing my weeping at the stars.

— anger (grief poems)

i am trying to remember you
and
let you go
at
the same time.

— the mourn

i think about winnie.
about
where she is living in her body right
now.
where she and madiba. are still in love.
in her neck.
in her spine.
in the ocean she is making with her eyes.

(how do you return the sun back to the sky. with someone. and let them leave you.)

— winnie

we
return to each
other
in waves.
this is how water
loves.

be easy.
take your time.
you are coming
home.
to yourself.

— the becoming | wing

NEJMA

BY NAYYIRAH WAHEED

precious.
is a word we barely know. but know we are not.
so then i say this to you.
you. with the low sun face. with the burning mountain eyes.
you. with the skin is that is always dusted with stars. you.
with the soil in your thigh. arm. lips.
you person of color.
you are precious.
you are precious.
you are precious.
spend time with this.

i am a soft revolution.
the one
whose hair is bleeding.

my mother gave me islam.
my father gave me the god of absence.
and here ii am.
a religion made of myself.

first.
anti.blackness: black is non.

second.
fetish: black non ness is. fascination. taboo. obsession. necessary consumption.

third.
exotic: the act of making black non ness acceptable. touchable. valuable.

fourth.
anti.blackness: black is non.

— the box circle

we are a slow golding soil.
opulent and starving.

— the black famine

i will hold this space for your return.
i will hold this space because
everyone of your lives. is our life.
this poem is searching for

You.
You.
You.
You.
You.
You.
You.
You.
You.
You.
You.
You.
You.
You.
You.
You.
You.
You.
You.
You.
You.
You.
You.
You.
You.

You.
You.
You.
You.
You.
You.
You.
You.
You.
You.
You.
You.
You.
You.
You.
You.
You.
You.
You.
You.
You.
You.
You.
You.
You.
You.
You.
You.

NEJMA

BY NAYYIRAH WAHEED

You.
You.
You.
You.
You.
You.
You.
You.
You.
You.
You.
You.
You.
You.
You.
You.
You.
You.
You.
You.
You.
You.
You.
You.
You.
You.
You.
You.

NEJMA

BY NAYYIRAH WAHEED

You.
You.
You.
You.
You.
You.
You.
You.
You.
You.
You.
You.
You.
You.
You.
You.
You.
You.
You.
You.
You.
You.
You.
You.
You.
You.
You.
You.

You.
You.
You.
You.
You.
You.
You.
You.
You.
You.
You.
You.
You.
You.
You.
You.
You.
You.
You.
You.
You.
You.
You.
You.
You.
You.
You.
You.

You.
You.
You.
You.
You.
You.
You.
You.
You.
You.
You.
You.
You.
You.
You.
You.
You.
You.
You.
You.
You.
You.
You.
You.
You.
You.
You.
You.

You.
You.
You.
You.
You.
You.
You.
You.
You.
You.
You.
You.
You.
You.
You.
You.
You.
You.
You.
You.
You.
You.
You.
You.
You.
You.
You.
You.

NEJMA

BY NAYYIRAH WAHEED

You.
You.
You.
You.
You.
You.
You.
You.
You.
You.
You.
You.
You.
You.
You.
You.
You.
You.
You.
You.
You.
You.
You.
You.
You.
You.
You.
You.

You.
You.
You.
You.
You.
You.
You.
You.
You.
You.
You.
You.
You.
You.
You.
You.
You.
You.
You.
You.
You.
You.
You.
You.
You.
You.
You.
You.

You.
You.
You.
You.
You.
You.
You.
You.
You.
You.
You.
You.
You.
You.
You.
You.
You.
You.
You.
You.
You.
You.
You.
You.
You.

this poem will find you.

— chibok. (the immutable measure of black life.)

what happens when
the war.
no. longer wants. war.

the cure for apathy is memory.

there is dark.
and
there is anti light.
these are not the same things.

the thing i know as poetry. is that feeling ii get in my eyes.

the first time i met my mother.
i knew she was not mine.

the house i grew up in was all ways sweating.
all. ways wet.
all. ways hot.
all. ways crying in another language.
this is why i'm this. malleable.
why
there is this. much. water in the blood.

— anemia

all the women.
in me.
are tired.

there is a god in writing.
a soft. roaring. unconditional. home of a god.
who prays to me.

i am mine.
before i am ever anyone else's.

— in

melanin is memory.
is the blue weight of the ocean.
sewn into the red dusk of sky. living in the soil of your body.
it is alive.
leaping and sweeping you. against.
into the sun.
your skin was the first astronaut.
the first in space.
you touch. talk. are intimate with the sun. everyday. and do not perish.

melanin.
is the world. before this world.
before the word. slave.
during the word. slave.
after the word. slave.
it is the books. written into yourself.
wild math in the pads of your feet.
soft science in your hair.
language down your back. invention in
your mouth.

melanin is why you are still alive.
after. the torching.
it is a second lung. the next heart. and the next heart. and the next.
a never ending. regenerative.
breathing thing.
a ceremony of life. while you are asleep.
a cosmos. in conversation.
immortal.

melanin is a wisdom that knew.
hate would be the anti light come to
devour. defile. destroy.
a wisdom that did not flinch.
a wisdom that is not bothered by such things.

melanin is memory.
future memory.
past memory.
your memory.
the memory of life. all.
in your skin.

— melanin

complexity is just simplicity which refuses to be anything else.

i will make you. on my back.
ii will raise you this way.
a child of the gravity. and the light.

— constellation

your father left. when you were in
the womb.
took his blood. and walked out the door.
while you were in the house of your mother.
in the house of your mother.
took his blood. when you needed it most.
if he could keep searching his hands. in the midst of your creation.
could hear you forming on your mother's life. on his life. and gather all his feet in secret.
all the other wild adventures of missing. he would drag you through. would only ever be this wound.
over and over and over again.
your father left. when you were in the womb.
took his blood. and walked out the door.
it would be the first and final. of all the leavings.

— all the leavings

mothers who leave.
for no other reason.
than
children are water in their throat.

— drown

there is a baby in my blood.
and
what am i to do.
my neck barely carries my head.
and
i don't have enough
to
hold a baby in.
what will become of my
small name.
my
little laughter
will they be filled
with
milk.
and
this water mountain (in my waist.)

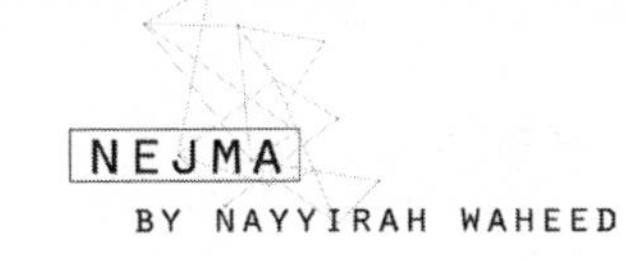

my sister says
i must say goodbye
to
my old voice.
(even though it is still hot from my mothers' pushing.)
she says
i must untie my tears from my eyes only at night.
she says
'lua, you will smell like a woman now.'
and
i am lost in the way
the sky
is falling
through her hands
as she tells me this.
there is a baby in my blood.
where
will i live.

— ten

if i give birth to twin poems.
a year apart from one other.
they may look as one person. but
they are really two.
two lives. breathing from the same mouth.

— two

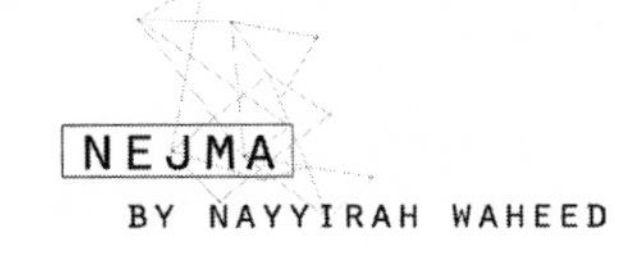

poetry
alters my dna.
every poem is a different life.
every poem brings me closer to myself. and breaks open a new future inside of me.

you want a romance with my blackness.
and how it holds you.
how it illuminates your skin. makes you break your
breath. against itself.
and how is this possible.
when your world has never made you breath. not once. ever. but my blackness
makes
you think about yourself. in a way you have never. and you are open. a question. alive. and now
hungry.

BY NAYYIRAH WAHEED

my blackness is your first love.
you are convinced it is. showing you what your eyes could 'never' see before. a 'world' bigger. brighter. dark. dusky and
wild. unashamed of itself. rebellious.
and it's cosmic. your relationship with how the night rolls off me into your hands.
you and my blackness are soul mates.
you met so
you could learn. more. expand.
because you always knew you were not like the others. who made sure they ate one white thing every day.
no. you
were
always uncomfortable with yourself.
you wear my culture around your neck. bask in and praise its jewels. pick it up on days when you want attention.
put it
down
when it starts
to stain. (you don't want to be disrespectful and take more than you should. you just want to be a part of something so beautiful.)

my blackness came to save you.
came to help you escape. the clutches of racism. of having that beast anywhere inside you. around you.
next to you.
your comfort. intimacy. proximity.
with my blackness
confirms. and affirms.
your nonracism. your lack of hate.
it is this heady trip. this painful awesome tryst. that brings you. flushed and moon eyed. to my door
with thank yous. and
i love yous. you have taught me to be a better person. you have changed my life.
but
this was never a relationship.
i have no idea who you are.
and i laugh
incredulous and insulted.
at the notion
that
my blackness could ever be your first love. that my blackness is your freedom.
that my blackness is yours.

— fetish

you will be black. again.
i will wait.

— anglophile

a poem can eat a person
whole.
for years.

i am taking a bath.
i am washing a war from me.

i need one year.
without
the dogs of whiteness.
trying
to devour me.

— the year (the unrelent)

'she is the dirty sea
in broken lingerie.'
i hear you say.
this.
as you throw and throw and throw ones down her throat.
and i think about how beautifully
her
skin guts you like a fish.
how she is warm gold on that pole.
and
the physics of her thighs.
the way she breaks
your eyes.
the home
her body makes for
your money. but not you. each and every night.
and
i think.
'you are the one
who is really in pain.'

— a dancer's thoughts one wednesday evening

on new years' day.
i woke.
showered. the old year into past life.
i fried calla lilies.
broke honeycomb over my feet.
drank water.
fed me.

— eating

the man who raps in flowers.

— andre benjamin

you are roasting
young honey leaves.
and
bright mango hearts. for our meal.
i bring you the bowls.
the quiet bowl.
the sour bowl.
the gold bowl.
the bowl that catches everything. missing nothing.
not one sigh. or laugh. or ache.
and just like this meal.
i am born from the palm of your hands. everyday.
hands that catch everything. that miss nothing.
not one sigh. or laugh. or ache.
hands that feel their way through me.
hands that break me open like limes.
the hands of akoul.

— akoul

when you are midnight.
i always know.
all the poignant blue freckle.
sweep across you.
you silver. then indigo. before completely becoming a war of stars.
it is the transformation of
human into sky
and
back again.

— yrsa's poem (this kind of human)

ocean.
the blue liquor.
the blue wine.

(that neverending nurturing you need.
the sea has it.)

every poem. here.
is an unwrite.
of all that has been written in me without. permission.

i will always be a translation.

teach you.
i cannot.
i am too busy making blood.

— privilege

as a black woman.
a woman of color.
writer.
artist.
creative.
my work is not a literary zoo.
for you to come observe. learn. about the animals.
or
a space to come and dissolve into a plastic empathy.
or a space to publicly. loudly. dominantly. flog your privileges.

nor is it
a warm. indiscriminate. cavernous. lap to lay in.

it is a boundary.
i am a boundary.

— unmammy

there were times
when i needed. no.
and
it was not there for me.

— the third parent

it is
the oldest anger.
the oldest anger.
the oldest anger.
in
the world.

i learned shukran. (thank you)
first.
shukran. (thank you) for this meal.
shukran. (thank you) for making this for me.
shukran. for everything.
and in the midst of all of this. gratitude.
la. (no)
was lost. before. i ever found it.

— the blunt force of gratitude

the way a poem bleaches everything the color of itself.
this is the way people stain.

— pomegranate

islam. is still in my life.
we are old soulmates.
who could not work out the knots against skin.
who could not believe in each other. while believing in ourselves.
who could not make each other happy. without.
making each other a sadness.
who
were born to each other. and never fell in love.
but
we still sip tea.
share our hands.
touch hearts.
every now and then.

— tea

so easily.
my
red mint tea.
becomes
a red mint sea.
and i am drinking a poem.

NEJMA

BY NAYYIRAH WAHEED

i have not written in months.
my fingers are molt.
you
are with a writer who is not
writing.

last night
you said 'love, let me read to you'

i was laying on my stomach
as you
began translating
the book of the fixed stars.
by
abd al-rahman al-sufi.
the persian. sufi. astronomer.

you said
'he handwrote this around 964.
a book of the sky. with his hands.'

we arrive at the page
where al-sufi speaks of a little cloud laying at the mouth of
a big fish.
('this was later named the andromeda galaxy' you say)

and as you read
i am transforming into that thing. i can feel it.
i am writing.
my stomach is writing.
my back is writing.
the water behind my right eye is writing.
i gather your hands to my lips.
i am grateful for you.
for the kind of love that will read me the (loosely translated) starworks
of incredible sufi astronomers on warm tuesday evenings.

(the kind of love that loves a writer when they cannot write.)

i am writing my way back to you.

you were born august 39th.
i was born on the 54th of april.

we are something.

born.
in
and
out of time.

i believe that everyone in the world.
has one poem.
that is their soulmate.

i was made from sex.
there is no shame. in such a creation.

— clean

when it comes. and it comes.
the sea hunger.
the blue fever.
a heat rash across my eyes and teeth.
you drive hours.
take an ice tray to the water.
bring it home. to freeze.
rub me down
with
pure ocean.
break the heat.

— seahydration

i walk into
a poem
and walk out someone else.

— writing

when writing.
there comes a time.
when you must let the writers you love. go.

whenever i think about
my mother and father. and the amount of
cruelty
i have ate at their
hands.
i remember that
i am the best of them.
and
i
am
at peace.

— redeem

don't give. it. to your children.
the thing.
that
was
given to you.

the
music
i knew as father.

— steveland morris

you must write. yourself.
before
you can write anything else.

we. are
the re.membering.

we have been lightcenturies away.

from ourselves.

but
now we are re.turn.ing

yes.
by love.

we are re.turn.ing.

— the re.membering

do not choose the lesser life.
do you hear me.
do you hear me.
choose the life that is. yours.
the life that is seducing your lungs.
that is dripping down your chin.

whether with a lover
or
none.
i reek of love.
i stink of love.

i want to keep our body above water.
you want to make us a fish.

— fish

a friend. is someone who supports your breath.

NEJMA

BY NAYYIRAH WAHEED

i see you.
training for rain.
burning oranges.
hoarding feathers beneath your clothes.
making a life a life.
and
i am reeling. from the glory. the power of you.

i lay all my lives onto the bed.
study my ornate geography.
taste all the wild planets i have made. and blush.

— a red map

NEJMA

BY NAYYIRAH WAHEED

our image.s.
always half.
always burning.
always welt.
always bent.
always garish.
always crawling.
always high.
always drunk.
always severed.
always flayed.
always vomiting.
always laughter laced with choking.
always chained.
always searing.
always stoic.
always monolith.
always ghetto.
always prisons.
always passive.
always stunted.

always begging.
always indifferent.
always deceit
always vicious.
always lazy.
always sex.
always abusive.
always abused.
always slave.
always adult from birth.
always child until death.
always pain.
always servant.
always at a mercy.
always unagency.
always aggressor.
always sadness.
always sinister.
always rabid.
always grasping.
always grabbing.

always razor blade.
always grotesque.
always apathetic.
always bloody.
always beast.
always body.
always regendered.
always misgendered.
always gendered.
always object.
always mammy.
always mule.
always mockery.
always accessories.
always vulgar.
always poverty.
always disgust. ing.
always whore.
always rage.
always blank.
always calculating.

always docile.
always stud.
always inept.
always killing.
always ugly.
always dumb.
always drugs.
always loathing.
always tragic.
always lurking.
always animal.
always respectable. politics.
always high white.
always fetish black.
always unpowered.
always hyperbolic.
always fear.
always on fire.
always impotent.
always destruction.
always spectacle.
always shatter.

always exacted into the perfect porn star.
to bring the world to orgasm.

— emotional porn (the black image industry)

i will.
and this will end.

— closure | dankyes

the prayers where we do not wish others well.
for all the brilliant. fetid. noxious. reasons.
the prayers we want to wash from the sky. as soon as they leave our imagination.
the ones born with no bones. so they leave no trace.
the harmful prayers. we pray.
because
we have been harmed.

we are forgiven those too.

— the soft law (forgiveness)

what is the word beyond. home.
after home.
where is it. this word.
why can i not remember how to say this
thing. this feeling that is my whole body.

give your creativity permission.
it's that simple, love.

i go.
with all the nothings.
all the myths.
and
all the flawings.
and return
full.
a new metal.
a waterlight.

— clothes made of water

i try to write with weight and air.
this way you
are held and set free at the same time.

the gold feeling.
that lives off the coast of your
body.
that is solid. and seething with light.

— the auric coast

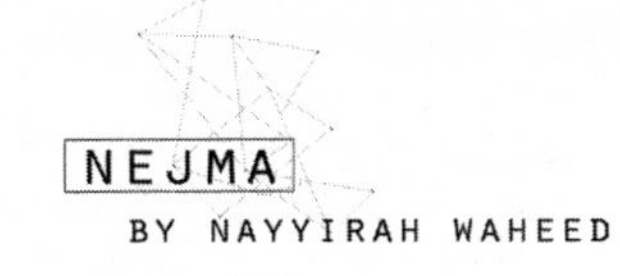

this book of thick stars.
this book is yours.

my work.
being housed
in the length.

the organ and wing.
of my people.

is the
only. shiny thing.
i need.

— the shortlist

i have a life to garden.
a multiverse to wake from sleep.

— giants

i have been wearing the ocean all day.

the blue dust.
the night. before the night.
the cinema of water. over water. over water.

— dusk

you are not racism.
you are not racism.
you are not racism.
you are not racism.
you are not racism.

your skin is not burden.
there is no mark against you.

your being is a holy beauty.

you.
are a holy beauty.

— ether

the first time
the mother saw it on her child.
she said

'no.
don't you dare.
you will not
grow up
thinking you are
unwanted. because your
father. chose. himself. over you.
this will not be your story
because it is not the truth.
the truth.
is.
your creation is not about him. not about me.
you came through us, my love. we were your vessel.
the truth is
you were born for you.
you were wanted by you.
you came for you.
you are here for you.
your existence is yours.
yes.
you will want him. (and on odd and warm nights he will think of you and hold himself tighter.)
but. what you do not get. from him.
does not make you less.
does not make you unwanted.
(trust that
all you did not receive. all you need. will come to you. in time. the universe is infinite.')

the first time
the mother saw it on her child.
she said

'no.
don't you dare.
you will not
grow up
thinking you are
unwanted. because your
mother. chose herself. over you.
this will not be your story
because it is not the truth.
the truth.
is.
your creation is not about her. not about me.
you came through us, my love. we were your vessel.
the truth is.
you were born for you.
you were wanted by you.
you came for you.
you are here for you.
your existence is yours.
yes.
you will want her. (and on odd and warm nights she will think of you and hold herself tighter.)
but. what you do not get. from her.
does not make you less.
does not make you unwanted.
(trust that
all you did not receive. all you need. will come to you. in time. the universe is infinite.')

the first time
they saw it on their child.
they said

'no.
don't you dare.
you will not
grow up
thinking you are
unwanted. because they.
chose themselves. over you.
this will not be your story
because it is not the truth.
the truth.
is
your creation is not about them. not about me.
you came through us, my love, we were your vessel.
the truth is
you were born for you.
you were wanted by you.
you came for you.
you are here for you.
your existence is yours.
yes.
you will want them. (and on odd and warm nights they will think of you and hold themselves tighter.)
but. what you do not get. from them.
does not make you less.
does not make you unwanted.
(trust that
all you did not receive. all you need. will come to you. in time. the universe is infinite.')

the first time
the father saw it on his child.
he said

'no.
don't you dare.
you will not
grow up
thinking you are
unwanted. because your
father. chose himself. over you.
this will not be your story
because it is not the truth.
the truth.
is
your creation is not about him. not about me.
you came through us, my love. we were your vessel.
the truth is
you were born for you.
you were wanted by you.
you came for you.
you are here for you.
your existence is yours.
yes.
you will want him. (and on odd and warm nights he will think of you and hold himself tighter.)
but. what you do not get. from him.
does not make you less.
does not make you unwanted.
(trust that
all you did not receive. all you need. will come to you. in time. the universe is infinite.')

the first time
the father saw it on his child.
he said

'no.
don't you dare.
you will not
grow up
thinking you are
unwanted. because your
mother. chose herself. over you.
this will not be your story
because it is not the truth.
the truth.
is
your creation is not about her. not about me.
you came through us, my love, we were your vessel.
the truth is
you were born for you.
you were wanted by you.
you came for you.
you are here for you.
your existence is yours.
yes.
you will want her. (and on odd and warm nights she will think of you and hold herself tighter.)
but. what you do not get. from her.
does not make you less.
does not make you unwanted.
(trust that
all you did not receive. all you need. will come to you. in time. the universe is infinite.')

the first time
the caregiver saw it on the child.
they said

'no.
don't you dare.
you will not
grow up
thinking you are
unwanted. because your
parents. chose themselves. over you.
this will not be your story
because it is not the truth. the truth. is your creation is not about them.
you came through them, my love, they were your vessel.
the truth.
is you were born for you.
you were wanted by you.
you came for you.
you are here for you.
your existence is yours.
yes.
you will want them. (and on odd and warm nights they will think of you and hold themselves tighter.)
but. what you do not get. from them.
does not make you less.
does not make you unwanted.
(trust that
all you did not receive. all you need. will come to you. in time. the universe is infinite.')

— a love poem (six ways)

just for tonight… just for tonight.
be the tenderest thing.
in the universe.

this whole book is weeping.
and
every pore of this book is joy.
and
that is the feast.